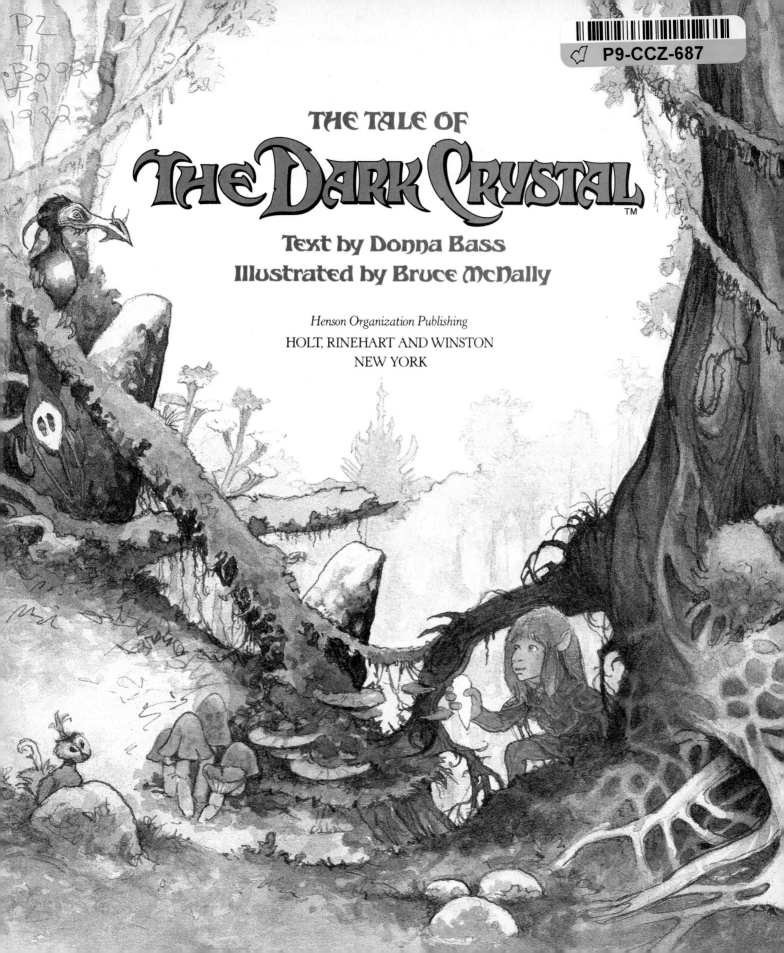

THE TALE OF
THE DARK CRYSTAL ™

Text by Donna Bass
Illustrated by Bruce McNally

Henson Organization Publishing

HOLT, RINEHART AND WINSTON
NEW YORK

THE TALE OF
THE DARK CRYSTAL

The Tale of the Dark Crystal
is based on the movie *The Dark Crystal* produced by Jim Henson and Gary Kurtz,
directed by Jim Henson and Frank Oz, with David Lazer as executive producer, screenplay
by David Odell and conceptual design by Brian Froud.

Published by Holt, Rinehart and Winston,
383 Madison Avenue, New York, New York 10017.
Published simultaneously in Canada by Holt, Rinehart and
Winston of Canada, Limited.

Library of Congress Cataloging in Publication Data
Bass, Donna.
The tale of the dark crystal.

Summary: On a faraway planet, Jen, the last of the
Gelflings, is given the mission of restoring a missing
shard to the great Crystal and preventing the tragedy of
a Skeksis triumph when the Three Suns merge.
[1. Science fiction. 2. Extraterrestrial beings—
Fiction]   I. McNally, Bruce, ill.   II. Title.
PZ7.B2927Tal   1982   [Fic]   82-11676

ISBN: 0-03-062414-2

Printed in the United States of America
3 5 7 9 10 8 6 4 2

ISBN 0-03-062414-2

1

Far away in time and space there was a world with Three Suns. Once this world was inhabited by the urSkeks, the Gelflings, and the Pod People, three different races. All were happy and free, living in the aura of a great, glowing Crystal that glittered from its many surfaces as brightly as a diamond.

Every thousand years the Three Suns would come together in a Great Conjunction. All that lived in the world would be renewed by the light that flooded down on them. But many years ago a terrible thing happened at the moment of the Great Conjunction. The urSkeks were split into two separate beings: the good and wise urRu, and the evil and cruel Skeksis. The Skeksis gained control of the Crystal and turned all that was good in their world into evil.

At the same time, the beautiful Crystal cracked and darkened. And dark it would remain until a piece that broke off—the crystal shard—was restored. According to an ancient Gelfling prophecy, the shard could be replaced only during the next Great Conjunction and only by the hand of a Gelfling. If the prophecy were not fulfilled, the power of the Skeksis would grow even stronger and their reign would be renewed forever.

The Skeksis did all they could to prevent the prophecy from coming true. They killed every Gelfling on the planet—or so they believed. The urRu had managed to save one Gelfling boy. They called him Jen, and they raised him secretly in a hidden valley, far away from the Skeksis. In all the years he was growing up, Jen knew no other place and spoke with no other beings but the urRu and the woodland creatures that also lived in the valley.

One day while Jen was playing his flute by his favorite pond, the sky became very dark, the wind started to howl, and the air grew sharply cold. Jen looked around and saw one of the urRu coming toward him.

"In your cave there is one who has need," the urRu said.

Wondering why urSu his Master needed him and frightened by the growing darkness, Jen hurried to his Master's side. He found urSu ready to go into the next world.

As urSu lay dying, he wanted to tell Jen about a special task that Jen, the last of the Gelflings, had to do.

"You are in danger, Gelfling….The rule of the Skeksis has brought forth pain," urSu gasped. He held his hand over the magic bowl and the liquid in the bowl formed itself into the shape of a piece of crystal.

"Mark well this crystal shard," urSu said. "On the Wall of Destiny it is written: A Gelfling must restore the shard to its rightful place. You are that Gelfling, Jen. You must heal the wound at the world's core. It is your only hope…of ending the rule of the Dark Crystal. Your journey must begin soon…for the Three Suns will not wait."

With those words, the shard disappeared. Jen heard it give off a musical sound as it vanished.

Jen did not understand what his Master was trying to tell him. But before he could ask urSu any questions, the Master's eyes closed, and his great head sank to rest. UrSu was dead.

Jen's heart was breaking. Alone and bewildered by urSu's last words, Jen left the cave.

At dawn, urSu was honored in a sacred urRu ceremony of song. Jen was there, mourning. One of the urRu then turned to Jen and told him that it was time to leave the valley.

"Very soon the Three Suns will become one. Unless by then you have found the future you must seek, and made what was broken whole, what was dark light, then darkness will be the fate of all creatures."

"But what am I to do? Where am I to go?" Jen asked.

"You must go to the high hill, to the dome of Aughra, Keeper of Secrets. In the end Aughra sees all."

Reluctantly, with fear and sadness in his heart, Jen did as the urRu said. He did not want to go, but he had been told he must. He looked back as he made his way up the path that wound out of the valley. The urRu, in their circle of stones, still sang at the funeral of urSu. They raised their heads and stared at Jen for a long time. It was their silent farewell. Jen stared back, then walked on toward the distant mountains.

2

IN the darkened castle of the Dark Crystal far from the valley of the urRu lived the Skeksis. Hooked and ugly, quarrelsome and unkind, the Skeksis were the same in number as the urRu, but their wicked opposites. Now only nine of each being remained. At the moment urSu had died, the Emperor of the Skeksis had died also.

Deep within the castle the Skeksis were bitterly arguing over who would be the next Emperor. Of all the Skeksis, the two most powerful were the Garthim-Master and the Chamberlain. Each disliked the other, and the rivalry for the throne was making that dislike even greater.

Suddenly the Garthim-Master looked at the Chamberlain, and shouting *"Haakskeekah!"* he challenged his hated enemy to a duel. As was the Skeksis custom, instead of striking each other with their swords, the two opponents struck at a large black stone. The first to shatter it would win both the duel and the Emperor's throne.

Grunting and groaning from the weight of their weapons, the Garthim-Master and the Chamberlain swung their ceremonial swords as they struggled to splinter the stone. The Garthim-Master, who was the stronger, was the first to do so. As he did, cheers of rejoicing met the new Emperor's ears.

The remaining Skeksis then surrounded the Chamberlain, tore his ornamental robes from him, and left him in tattered rags.

All at once a cry "The Crystal!" echoed through the castle. The Skeksis turned their backs on the disgraced Chamberlain and rushed frantically to the Crystal Chamber, talking excitedly, pushing and pulling at each other rudely.

Suspended in midair at the chamber's center was the Dark Crystal. Once clear and glowing, it now gave off a dark, unnatural light. The Crystal had never healed, so it remained cracked and decaying.

Now the Skeksis could see, pictured in the Crystal, an image of Jen climbing a steep cliff on his journey toward Aughra's dome. He had been spotted by the Skeksis' spying Crystal Bats. In their claws they grasped seeing crystals, which had beamed Jen's picture back to the Crystal in the castle.

The Skeksis were filled with panic at what they saw. They thought they had killed every Gelfling. But now it seemed that one Gelfling was still alive, and a live Gelfling could destroy them all.

"Garthim! Garthim!" The Garthim-Master screamed at once for his army of

monstrous soldiers. The Garthim were like huge dark beetles, armored, hard, and heavy.

Looking at the picture of Jen deep inside the Crystal, the Garthim-Master hoarsely commanded his Garthim, "Kill it! Kill the Gelfling!"

Immediately the Garthim, creatures of destruction, clattered out of the castle, followed by a rattling swarm of Crystal Bats.

Lurking in a darkened corner of the chamber, the Chamberlain could also see the image of Jen. He turned and left the castle alone, going the same way as the Garthim, in pursuit of the Gelfling.

UNAWARE of what was happening at the Skeksis' castle, Jen trudged on over grassy plains, across shallow streams, and finally climbed up a steep, jagged cliff. As he looked around for the dome of Aughra,

roots and branches of a tree shot out in front of him. They wrapped themselves around him and pulled him up into the air. Frightened, Jen struggled helplessly. Suddenly the branches parted, and an unblinking eye held in a twisted hand was staring at him. Startled, Jen stared back. The eye vanished, then reappeared on the most terrifying face Jen had ever seen, and the face belonged to an even more strange and terrifying being.

"You Gelfling?" she asked in disbelief.

"I am," Jen answered. His voice trembled with fear.

"Can't be. All dead."

"I am not dead. I am Jen the Gelfling," Jen told her. "Are you Aughra, Watcher of the Heavens?"

"Who sent you? What you want?"

"UrSu my Master showed me a vision of your dome. Then another vision of a crystal shard. I do not undersand what he was telling me to do, but if I can find the shard I might—"

"That all?" Aughra cackled. "Why not say so? Follow!"

Aughra gently touched the branches, and they lowered Jen to the ground. He then ran after Aughra, into a dark tunnel that led to her Observatory.

Beneath a dome that glowed with a golden light Jen stopped, dazzled by the whirling discs and rods whizzing by him. This was an enormous model of the Three Suns and their planets, all of them turning, spinning, with moons and comets rising and falling, swooping down and around. Jen had to keep dodging the moving worlds to avoid being knocked over. Aughra knew all the movements and ducked out of the way without even looking. It all made Jen dizzy. Never had he dreamed of anything so wonderful. Never had the urRu told him there were such things.

"Suns, planets, moons," said Aughra. "Everything in the heavens. How else you know about conjunctions? Big one coming up. Better be underground for that one. Whole planet might burn up."

"What's a conjunction?" Jen asked, jumping out of the way of a razor-sharp moon.

"The Great Conjunction. When the Three Suns become one. Soon. The end of the world. Or the beginning." Aughra laughed. "UrRu. They not tell you anything?"

"Oh, many things. But not about this." Jen dove to the floor as a great comet whizzed by.

Aughra looked at him for a long time. Then she started to tell him about the Skeksis and Garthim, the shard and the Dark Crystal. But what she told him only made him more confused. And frightened him, too. He guessed that whatever he was supposed to do would be very dangerous.

Aughra opened a cabinet and took out a box full of pieces of crystal. Jen gazed at the shards. How would he know which one to pick? He decided to try to find the one that most looked like the shard he had seen in the magic bowl.

Finally, he was left with three. But they all looked the same. Then he remembered the sound he had heard in the cave as the shard disappeared. Jen picked up his flute and sounded that note. As he played, one of the shards began to glow and sounded the same note back. Jen picked up the shard and stared at it, happy that he had found it and curious about what it all meant.

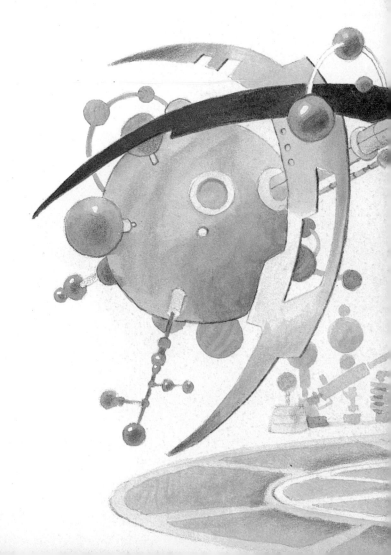

Suddenly, Jen heard a terrible clicking noise. Giant black claws were ripping open a wall of the Observatory. Through that hole the Garthim came, smashing their way toward Jen.

Jen jumped up, terrified. He shoved the shard into his pocket. The Garthim were only a few yards away…and there was no escape! Above, a giant metal moon dipped toward him. He did the only thing he could do. He leaped onto the table and ran toward the moon. As it swooped down, Jen hurled himself into the air and wrapped his arms around it. Up, up, up they swung, over the snapping claws of the Garthim, higher and higher, toward the top of the dome. Looking down, Jen saw the table catch fire and the flames begin to spread.

Jen knew that at any moment the moon

would begin to descend. Swinging his legs he threw himself against the wall of the dome, hoping to land on the ledge. But the wall cracked open, and Jen somersaulted through the air, landed, and tumbled head over heels down a steep, rocky hillside. He finally came to a stop at the foot of the hill. He stood up a bit dazed and brushed himself off. He was bruised and cut in several places, but at least he was safe. And so was the shard.

Above him the dome burst into flames with a roar. Jen sighed, thinking of Aughra, then ran into the forest. The only one to see him go was the Chamberlain. He was too far away to catch Jen. But he turned and struggled slowly through the thick, jungly bushes in pursuit of the Gelfling.

4

DEEP in the forest, strange cries of woodland creatures kept Jen awake all night. Everything was new to him, and he was afraid. By daylight he wandered through the swampland, peering cautiously around bushes and through branches. At the sudden sound of growling, Jen spun around. Staring out at him from inside a tree trunk a ferocious furry face opened its mouth, bared its many rows of pointed teeth, and let out a terrible roar. Jen jumped back in fright and fell into the muddy pool behind him. Then he heard laughter. He looked up and could not believe what he saw.

Standing before him was a girl of his own age. Her hair was long and fair, her eyes large and grey. Like Jen she had wide cheekbones, a small chin, and pointed ears.

"Are you Gelfling?" Jen finally asked.

"Yes," she answered.

"But…I thought I was the only one."

"So did I."

They smiled at each other, surprised and delighted.

"I have been hidden all my life with the Pod People in their village near here," she said. "I am Kira."

"I am Jen."

The fuzzy thing with teeth scurried out to hide behind Kira. To Jen's relief, the face belonged to a tiny ball of fur, nothing more. Kira introduced it as her pet, Fizzgig. She then reached out her hand to Jen's. But when their hands touched, a strange thing happened.

Without words each of them saw into the memories of the other's mind: Each had been rescued from a village destroyed by Garthim; each had been raised by the beings who had rescued them. Jen learned about Kira and Fizzgig, Kira learned about Jen and the shard.

Kira helped Jen out of the pool, and their hands parted.

"How did we talk without speaking?" Jen asked.

"Dreamfasting," Kira explained. She then invited Jen to come home with her to meet the Pod People.

They journeyed downriver in the shell of a giant beetle. Around them were the musical sounds of the forest. Jen was no longer afraid, now that Kira was with him.

Kira suddenly pushed Jen down in the boat, grabbed for her hunting thong, and flung it directly above their heads. There was flapping, squawking, splashing. Then silence.

"I spotted a Crystal Bat," Kira whispered. "They spy for the Skeksis. What they see with their crystals, the Skeksis see, too. I don't think it saw us."

But Kira was wrong. It was too dark for her to see that the Crystal Bat was not dead, only wounded. From the water it pointed its crystal at the Gelflings.

Far away from the river the urRu knew it was time for them to leave the valley. Dressed in their dusty garments and leaning heavily on their walking sticks, they followed one after the other, up the path and across the plain.

Finally, Jen, Kira, and Fizzgig arrived at Pod Village. Kira was much loved here; and the cheerful little Pod People, led by Ydra, Kira's foster mother, welcomed her home with much joy. But they were confused by Jen's arrival. They had thought that Kira was the only Gelfling alive, but now it seemed there were two. When they saw how happy Jen and Kira were, they smiled and welcomed Jen also. Then the merrymaking began.

There was eating and drinking and laughing and singing. The music grew faster and faster, and some of the Pod People began to dance. Jen looked at Kira and thought he had never been so happy or felt so much at home. He did not have to dreamfast to know she felt the same way.

"How long can we stay here?" Jen asked.

"As long as we want."

"Then I don't ever want to go," Jen said.

"But what about the crystal shard?" Kira asked with concern.

"I just want to stay with you."

The band struck up again, and Ydra asked Jen to dance. Shyly he agreed. The house was soon shaking with shouting and clapping and singing and dancing.

And then a hideous noise filled the air as a huge black claw suddenly slashed through a side of the house, sending splinters flying. Through the hole Garthim battered their way in, overturning chairs and tables in their path. Howling in terror, the Pod People scattered in all directions, crashing into each other in their desperate attempt to escape destruction. Some did escape; others did not. Still others were seized by Garthim claws and stuffed into a cage to be taken back to the castle, there to become slaves.

Jen ran toward Kira. "It's us they're after!" he cried, ducking behind the table where Kira and Fizzgig were hiding. She nodded. Her eyes were fastened on a Garthim only a few feet away.

Jen pulled the shard out of his pocket. As the Garthim grabbed his arm, he stabbed wildly at the black thing with his free hand. The shard pierced the Garthim's claw and a note sang out that could be heard all over the land. Far away the urRu, slowly making their way to the castle of the Skeksis, heard it too.

Wounded, the Garthim let go of Jen and pulled away. Jen, too, was hurt, and blood flowed from his arm.

Jen grabbed Kira's hand. With Fizzgig at their heels, they found their way out of the house and raced toward the forest, toward safety.

Every house in the village had been destroyed, smoke was everywhere, and the cries of the Pod People filled the air.

Jen and Kira had no time to stop and stare in sorrow. Clattering and pounding in close pursuit were several Garthim. At any moment the Gelflings expected one of them to clutch them from behind and crush them to death.

Suddenly, the Chamberlain stepped out from behind the trees where the forest began. He raised his hand. The Garthim stopped their pursuit, paused, then turned back to the village. The Chamberlain turned to watch the Gelflings escape into the forest.

5

DEEP into the forest's darkness Jen and Kira fled, not stopping until they were safe. Both were filled with sadness over the destruction of Pod Village. Jen, feeling he was to blame, angrily threw the shard away into the night.

When morning came, Jen saw that they had been sleeping near beautiful remains of what had once been a village. He walked closer to one of the buildings, feeling very drawn to what was inside.

"Don't, Jen," Kira warned. "I was told never to enter."

"I have to see what's inside," Jen insisted as he stepped through the doorway.

Hesitant but curious, Kira followed, clutching Fizzgig close to her. As she did, she knelt down to pick up the shard Jen had thrown away the night before. It was lying on the ground, pointing toward the old building.

Jen and Kira found themselves in a large, musty room. Light was streaming down through holes in the ruined roof; dead leaves, mold, and moss blanketed the floor; and scraps of tattered faded fabric hugged the walls. In the next room on one of the far walls were wonderful wall carvings and drawings telling the history of the Gelfling race. And Jen read the written words to Kira:

> *When single shines the Triple Sun,*
> *What was sundered and undone*
> *Shall be whole, the two made one,*
> *By Gelfling hand, or else by none.*

At last Jen understood what he must do. He must be at the castle at the time of the Great Conjunction, when the Three Suns would meet as one, to heal the wound in the Crystal with the missing shard. Excited and determined, Jen smiled at Kira as she handed him the shard he had thrown away.

A shadow suddenly fell across them. There standing before them was a Skeksis in tattered rags, smiling at them.

"Stay," the Chamberlain pleaded, raising his taloned hand. "Am friend to Gelfling. Save you from Garthim. Am I enemy?"

"What do you want with us?" Jen asked, though Kira begged him not to listen.

"Come with me to castle. I show Skeksis you want peace and will not harm us. Skeksis afraid of prophecy that Gelflings end Skeksis rule. Peace bring end to Skeksis slaughter of Gelflings. Please." The Chamberlain reached out his hand as if in friendship.

Jen was drawn to the Skeksis' wheedling voice, but Kira did not trust the creature. Tugging on Jen's arm she cried, "No, Jen!" and pointed to the carvings of the Gelfling destruction by the Garthim.

Jen knew Kira was right. He grabbed her hand and fled through an open window.

The Chamberlain watched them go, knowing where they were headed.

Jen, Kira, and Fizzgig darted through the forest. The meeting with the Chamberlain had only strengthened Jen's determination to make the prophecy come true, to heal the Crystal's wound. He glanced up into the sky. The light seemed strange to him. With a sinking heart he realized that the Great Conjunction was rapidly approaching and the future of all creatures depended on his reaching the castle in time.

Coming to a clearing, they paused. Kira uttered a string of insectlike chirps and clicks, and four Landstriders, strange long-legged beasts, creamy in color, with long whiskers, appeared. Kira jumped joyfully onto the back of one of the creatures, and Fizzgig nestled down happily inside her pocket.

"Don't be afraid," Kira reassured Jen, who looked worried. "They'll take us wherever I ask them."

"You don't have to go," Jen told her after struggling onto the back of another Landstrider.

"I know," she replied quietly. She then turned and they were off at an incredible speed, racing across a wide plain, up hills and down, over streams, onward to the castle.

Finally, they came to the crest of a cliff. Looking over it, they saw a ravine surrounding the castle, and beyond that the castle itself. Trudging toward it were the Garthim returning from the raid on Pod Village. They carried a cage crowded with wailing Pod captives.

Kira clicked her tongue, and the Landstriders sprinted down the steep rocky slope and crashed into the Garthim. Jen and Kira were thrown but not harmed. While the Landstriders bravely fought the black monsters, the Gelflings ran toward the cage, hoping to set the Pod captives free.

Kira shouted, "Jen!" as she began to tear at the cage. Inside was Ydra, her face crushed against the bars. "Don't worry," Kira was saying, "we'll get you out!" But there was not enough time. The Landstriders, greatly outnumbered by the Garthim, had been destroyed, and the Garthim were in pursuit of Jen and Kira.

The Gelflings were on the edge of the ravine and had nowhere to run, nowhere to hide. Just as menacing Garthim claws grasped at them, Kira wrapped her arms around Jen and, with Fizzgig on her shoulder, jumped into the ravine.

But they did not fall! Instead, they floated gently through the air. To Jen's amazement, a pair of wings had unfolded from Kira's back.

"Once, ages ago, all girl Gelflings could fly—not just flutter down to the ground," Kira explained as they landed safely at the bottom of the ravine.

Jen and Kira looked around. Mountains of garbage filled the gully with an awful smell. They walked on until they found what seemed to be an entrance through the castle sewers. Kira shuddered at the sight.

"There's no other way," Jen said.

Kira nodded. "I know."

Then they crawled into the tunnel.

The Chamberlain, watching from above the ravine, smiled and turned toward a hidden entrance to the castle.

6

SLIME covered the walls of the dimly lit tunnel, and unseen creatures slithered along the ground. As Jen and Kira stumbled on their way, a shadow once again crossed their path.

"I knew you would come," the Chamberlain said with a smile. "We make peace now."

"No!" Kira cried as he grabbed them, one in each hand, and headed toward the castle.

Wriggling his arms free, Jen slid the shard from his pocket and, with all his strength, plunged it into the Chamberlain's arm. The shard gave off a blinding flash. The Chamberlain cried out in pain and dropped Jen.

In the wilderness one of the urRu held up his arm. It was bleeding where a deep cut had suddenly appeared. In the sky, the Three Suns were moving closer to each other.

Grasping a beam that supported the roof, the Chamberlain pulled it down and the roof caved in, burying Jen beneath stone and rock. Kira cried to Fizzgig to stay with Jen as the Chamberlain dragged her to the Council Chamber.

There the Skeksis were awaiting the moment of the Great Conjunction, when their strength and their reign would be renewed.

Beaming with triumph, the Chamberlain entered the room and flung the Gelfling girl onto the floor before them. The Skeksis gasped in horror. A live Gelfling! What should they do with it? The Garthim-Master ordered that Kira be imprisoned in the Scientist's laboratory, the Chamber of Life. As Kira was dragged away, the Garthim-Master turned to the Chamberlain and awarded him new robes and his old office.

Kira was terribly frightened by the sights and sounds of the Chamber of Life. The Scientist sat her in a chair and clamped her to it so she could not move.

"Jen, help me!" Kira called out.

Her terrified cry was heard by Jen deep inside the tunnel. He stirred beneath the rocks, groaning and calling back, "Kira! Fight them!"

Then an old woman's voice cried out from a cage, "Call out, Gelfling! You have powers. Use them. Speak to those who are here with you. Stronger than Skeksis they are, all together, if you speak to them."

Kira looked around and saw hundreds of woodland creatures staring at her through the bars of their cages. She threw back her head, and in their language she cried out to them to break out of their cages and be free. In answer they screeched and howled, throwing themselves against their cages in a growing frenzy until finally they were free. Then they attacked the Scientist. Birds flew up and flapped in his face; animals of the wild lunged at his feet. Flailing his arms as he lost his balance, the Scientist tripped and plunged through an opening, falling into the pit of fire below.

At that moment, as the urRu were approaching the castle, the Alchemist disappeared. Only eight urRu and eight Skeksis now remained.

Struggling out of the clamp that held her to her chair, Kira ran over to the old woman and swung open her cage. It was Aughra.

"Too late, Gelfling. Very soon Three Suns begin to touch. Skeksis get much power. No one can fight them. All is lost...unless you have shard."

"Jen has it! I must find Jen!" Kira cried and ran out of the chamber.

Still struggling, Jen crawled out from under the rocks. With Fizzgig at his heels he was carefully making his way toward Kira and the Dark Crystal. Suddenly he fell through a trapdoor and landed on a cold stone floor. Jen was afraid. He reached for the shard, which faintly glowed in the darkness. At once the large shapes Jen could almost see started to make a familiar clicking noise and opened gleaming purple eyes. Garthim! Lumbering toward Jen, they collided with each other, and one of them crashed through the wall behind him. Quickly Jen darted through the hole and inched his way up a stone shaft lit by a pit of fire below. High above him floated the Dark Crystal.

With the last of his strength Jen pulled himself through the opening at the top of the shaft and found himself in the Chamber of Life. There he saw Aughra.

"No time! 'When single shines the Triple Sun,'" Aughra warned him. "Hurry and find your friend!"

Jen dashed from the chamber.

Outside the castle the Three Suns were almost touching the sky. The urRu, chanting, had reached the castle entrance, which was guarded by Garthim. But the Garthim did not move. They had been lulled into a trance by the urRu's song.

Inside the castle, Jen, desperately looking for
Kira, ran along corridors and up staircases,
until he came to a high balcony overlooking
the Dark Crystal. Being so close to the Crystal
at last, seeing its glory, sensing its power, and
understanding the meaning of his mission,
Jen was overwhelmed with awe.

Then he looked up. High above the Dark
Crystal was an open window. Through it Jen
could see the Three Suns, touching but not yet
one. The shard he held in his hand pulsed and
glowed. Then he looked down. The Skeksis,
dressed in their ceremonial robes, were
marching solemnly into the Crystal Chamber
and moving to their positions of power around
the base of the Crystal. A choir of Pod slaves
had taken their places in readiness for the
ceremony. Among them was Ydra.

Jen's gaze then drifted to the balcony
opposite when, suddenly, Kira appeared.
Their eyes met and they silently rejoiced at
seeing each other alive.

At that moment Fizzgig joyfully found
Kira. He too had been wandering through the
castle looking for her. Now he was barking and
jumping up and down to let her know how
happy he was.

The Garthim-Master heard the barking and, seeing Kira on one side of the balcony and Jen on the other, screamed, "Garthim! Gelfling!"

The Garthim outside the chamber door stampeded through the castle corridors toward Jen and Kira.

As the Garthim closed in on him, Jen inched closer to the edge of the balcony and then, with shard in hand, leaped onto the Crystal just out of reach of Garthim claws. Frantically he grappled for a hold on the slippery surface. He succeeded in clinging fast, but the shard slipped from his fingers and fell,

like a spinning sliver of light, landing on the very edge of the shaft that led to the pit below.

In the silence that followed, Kira leaped from the balcony and fluttered down on her spread wings. Fizzgig, seeing her leaving again, raced down the staircase to the chamber floor. All the Skeksis moved toward the shard, and the Garthim-Master was the first to reach it. As he leaned over to pick it up, Fizzgig, wanting to help Kira, bit the Skeksis' arm. The Garthim-Master snarled with pain and flapped his arm angrily. Fizzgig was thrown off-balance and vanished down the shaft.

Darting in between the Skeksis, Kira snatched the shard. The Skeksis shrank back from her in fear. Holding the shard out in front of her, Kira slowly turned around the circle of Skeksis that had surrounded her.

In the opening above the Dark Crystal the Three Suns overlapped.

The Chamberlain, with outstretched hand, came forward. "Give me shard, Gelfling. And you go in peace."

"Don't hurt her!" Jen shouted to the Chamberlain. "You can have it! Let her go!"

"No, Jen! Heal the Crystal!"

She turned her face to him. He was crying, "No, Kira! They'll kill you!" as she threw the shard back up to him.

Reaching out he caught it. Then he looked down and screamed as the Ritual-Master struck her from behind. Kira fell to the floor.

Jen turned to face the sky. He could not see. A brilliant beam of light flooded down, bathing him and the Crystal in blinding brightness. The Three Suns were one.

With tears streaming down his cheeks, Jen raised his arm and plunged the shard deep into the wound of the Crystal.

The Crystal flashed. With the flash came a high-pitched bell-like boom of thunder. Jen was thrown from the Crystal and fell through the dazzled air. He landed unharmed and ran over to Kira's lifeless body. Cradling her in his arms, he sobbed with grief.

Around him the light of the great Crystal, no longer darkened by its wound, was clear and glowing. The bodies of the Garthim were cracking and falling apart. The Pod slaves, including Ydra, were free. The filthy walls of the castle were crumbling, revealing its original pure crystal beauty. The evil reign of the Skeksis was over.

Into the brilliant chamber came the urRu, no longer weary but with strength renewed. They formed a circle around the Crystal, each standing in a pool of light, each chanting a song of truth and majesty. Writhing and hissing, each Skeksis was drawn to its urRu counterpart.

Aughra hobbled into the Crystal Chamber, Fizzgig in her arm. She had rescued him as he was falling down the shaft. Together they made their way to the Crystal Chamber and watched as urRu and Skeksis merged into a single being, the urSkeks. As in the past, the two were one.

Through his sobbing, Jen heard a voice speak. He looked up into the wise gaze of the urSkek figure towering above him.

"Gelfling, you have freed us from this world to return to the next. Now we can return the favor. You restored the true power of the Crystal. Make your world in its light." The urSkek then touched Kira's shoulder, healing her wound. She opened her eyes. Holding each other, Jen and Kira watched as the urSkeks were drawn into the Crystal on beams of light.

Jen smiled. At last he truly understood urSu's message. By healing the wound in the Crystal, Jen had restored harmony and goodness to the world. And now all the creatures could live in peace.